THE
LAMPREY

IN THE WAKE OF PASSION

Published by Susa Pflug
Translated by Kevin Oakes

FSC
www.fsc.org
MIX
Papier aus ver-
antwortungsvollen
Quellen
Paper from
responsible sources
FSC® C105338

Herstellung und Verlag:
BoD – Books on Demand, Norderstedt
ISBN: 978-3-7481-7910-8

1

Paul dropped back onto his couch with a deep sigh of relief. It had gone better than he had hoped. The music outside drifted into his office. The Christmas party, which was coming to an end, had definitely been a success.

What a stroke of genius it had been! Right in the middle of the first speech he had made after the death of his mother, to stop shortly and then, amazed at his own courage, smiling inwardly to continue with:

„You know what. For a whole year we've worked hard and often got on one another's nerves. So, why should I reprimand you here and now with balances and threats and ruin our Christmas Party?"

„We just sang „O Du Fröhliche" (O Joyous One) so, let's be joyous and merry."

„Let's do it. Merry Christmas!"

Thunderous applause. Up till now the obligatory Christmas carols were followed by the obligatory Christmas speech, spiced with appeals, demands and threats, or, the company would be forced to close, a real party pooper. But not tonight, tonight was different, „O Du Fröhliche".

The employees, almost a hundred of them, consisting mainly of women, were „over the moon" and cheered their „liberator". To save money, the party was held in the firm, but Paul saw to it that a small combo got everyone in the mood. At first the trio played the obligatory Christmas carols, then German folksongs and finally well known hits and hot dance rythms. Everyone was dancing, no one had a choice! And so did Paul. But, he still had to process the sorrow of the loss of his stern mother and boss. Thus he had resisted the temptation for a long time tonight. But of course he let himself be softened up for one little dance. First he danced with the assembly line manageress and then with the workers union chairwoman. After that everyone wanted to dance with him.

It was great fun. But right in the middle of this tumult, his „head shaking mother" appeared in his intoxicated imagination

„Paul?"

With an „I have to", Paul snuck out of the canteen.

Paul, then alone in his office, with the music in his ears and feeling happy about the success of the evening, stretched out his limbs and promptly fell asleep.

Paul dreamt. He dreamt of the things that his mother, with her „Paul, one doesn't do that", had managed to manipulate his life. No wonder that Paul was not only still single, to say nothing of a lack of experience in love. Now he was free and so were his dreams.

He lay on a padded lounger in the sample room of the department store „Kaufhof", surrounded by super, long legged, well-trained lady buyers. Tired from buying and drunk with successful sales, the lady buyers moved in on him. Especially the „Circe" from the lingerie department, who had up to now turned down his offers, she now began to audaciously inspect the manly contents of his pants. The sorceress had hardly taken possesion of the object of her desire, a tender kiss and then she began to quietly suck. His small mannikan grew and grew. Through the skilled use of hands and lips, his previously unused penis took on an enormous form. A brand new excitement rushed through his body. Paul's breathing became heavier and shorter. He was highly aroused.

Paul woke up. It wasn't a dream. Was it some cruel reality?! He was shocked, almost in a trance, when he noticed that it wasn't the lady buyer from the lingerie department in Kaufhof. It was Rita, his employee from the final-check department.

„Stop it! What do you think you're doing?!"

Paul tried to apply lifelong aquired principles of upbringing – all in vain.

Rita was lying heavily and immovably on his hip!

„This is an unprecedented outrage!"

This in no way distracted Rita from her intensive activity. But it did result in Rita taking a small break and whispering the following explanation.

„Psst......quiet boss, quiet. The others don't have to know. It's me, Rita from the final-check department.You were so nice today, and also a little bit sad. I saw you sneaking out of the hall and didn't want to leave you alone. I waited in front of your office for a while and then I came in to look for you. And what did I see? Your bulging pants. And I thought to myself, as our boss has given us so much pleasure this evening, he shouldn't miss out on a bit of pleasure himself, as he was having his in his sleep. The others out there are already at it.!"

Paul shuddered to think of his whole company out there fucking.

Rita tolerated no objection and showed no mercy.

She now took the slightly shrivelled „man-toy" between her lips, while her gentle tongue pushed back the foreskin to play around the head, which made paul's „little-man" start to grow again.

„You see, he's having fun!"

Wild thoughts ran through Paul's mind

„It's too late now, I can't move, what do I do now, oh, who gives a shit, it's wonderful, it's fucking amazing, it's...it'ssss.... ii...sssss!"

Then with a vehement outburst „Yeaaaahh" and „Oh God, oh God, oh God" was followed by Paul's ejaculation, like a grenade exploding. Stars flashing through his brain, then a short darkness. Paul's body was enjoying the climax. Paul jerked heavily a few times as Rita kept sucking and slurping.

He groaned quietly:

„Stop, stop, it's hurting."

Paul came back to reality.

„Oh God, oh God, my pants."

Rita let go of Paul's dick for the first time.

„Boss, haven't I learned from you, haven't you taught us all."

„Everyone leaves their workplace as they found it, clear and clean!"

Paul is perplexed.

„Yes but where did you put it?"

Rita laughed softly.

„Where? Where to? Down my throat."

Paul shuddered for the second time.

„Can one swallow that stuff, just like that?"

Rita enlightened her boss in her own drastic way.

„Well, I tried it once with my boyfriend. But, it smelt so weird and then when Í had it in my throat, I felt like puking – it was disgusting. I had to spit it out. My boyfriend sneeringly told me „don't be so dramatic!" So, I broke up with him."

And then, almost admiringly:

Í'm baffled at the huge amount you produce. Haven't done it in a while huh?"

Paul realised that he was nodding. Rita continued in her vulgar slang.

„Boss, I have to say that your juice not only smells nice, it tastes good too!"

Rita stopped for a second.

„It tastes great, yeah, it has a nutty flavour, vanilla and nuts, I could just about do it again....!"

„Don't you dare! Stop now!"

„Too bad, don't be mad Boss, I'll be off. And merry Christmas, that was a real surprise, what with the Christmas party and the egg liquer with almond!"

Lost in thought, Paul added:

„Vanilla with nuts."

Paul wanted to warn Rita to be quiet and keep this between them and explain more. But Rita was already out of the office, just as quick as she had entered it. A full five minutes later, Paul was still confused about what had happened. Dream or reality? His thoughts kept being crossed by Rita's hands and tongue. He got tired and eventually fell peacefully asleep in those same pants that Rita had neatly buttoned up for him. Three hours later Paul tiptoed out of the building (why so secretly?).

The building was empty by now. The cleaning ladies would come tomorrow morning. The caretaker had found Paul sleeping during his last round, but had left him sleeping there.

2

„Hello Shark?“

„Hello Paul, yes Shark here.“

„Did you have a good Christmas?“

„Can't really say „good“. No, sleeping and mainly alone.“

„It is not good that man should be alone! Moses 2:18.“

„Yes dear altar boy Paulus, well observed! But, was God's advice for the then exisiting humanity, consisting of Adam really good? After the catastrophe of my last relationship, abstinence is the only truth!“

„Once again a question of truth?“

„Paul, there you stand all alone, and I am far from having some girlfriend pussy, so I don't see much difference!“

„I see one: You're hanging in there like a sick man being drip fed, while a woman happily made me drip!“

„Hey Paul, what do Ihear, what's up with you? I'm astounded: you nailed someone.“

„Why so vulgar?“

„It's just jealousy! There I am spending a dry time under the Christmas tree and you have hardly escaped your mother's disciplinary rules, when you start acting the playboy. What happened? How was it?“

„Not the way you imagine it!“

„Have you turned gay? Did you do it from behind?“

„Shark, behave yourself!“

Paul's memories were on the tip of his tongue, so he spilt his adventure like a filibuster it's treasures. Surprisingly Shark seemed to be disappointed.

„Oh, I see, only fellatio? Paul every horny girl does that. Every slut and every nun!"

„So sorry, but I'm neither nun nor slut!"

„That's true. The only french you know is from school! You're missing the practice. Crazy! How can one speak with their mouth full? And then in „French"?"

„Can't you be serious for once? You've spoilt my mood."

„Fine! Then let me ask you concretely: Colleague? Minor? A sexual offence with dependants? Handcuffs, all screwed up, or were you lucky, and she was of age? How old is your sexworker?"

„About thirty."

„Now come on tell me, is she pretty?"

„Yeah, I suppose so, a good figure, friendly and a reliable worker."

„But, what do you mean by"I suppose so"?"

„Well, she would be really pretty if she had a clear skin. She has too many pimples."

„Then it was a good thing that the room was cloaked in darkness."

„Shark, are pimples contagious?"

„Not that I know of. Imagine if you had a dick with pimples: a pickled prick (pimpled dick?), shortly „Pickleprick"!" (*Pimpledick*)

Shark laughed tongue in cheek pleased with his imagination.

„You know what Paul, it's not that bad. The only thing worrying me is: will she keep her mouth shut? Will she tell her colleagues?"

„Once your reputation is ruined"....or maybe not? Women think differently. Maybe some hush money will keep her quiet! You must watch her on the first day back at work. Call her into your office immediately."

3

Shark's worries came to pass, shortly after the phone call. It was during the first week back at work after Christmas. Paul hadn't found any time to talk to Rita and had a bad concience. On the otherhand he was calmed by the fact that during the daily workplace checks, Rita had not, in the smallest way dropped any hints about their rendezvous. It was already Friday. Weekend. The usual hectic spread through the firm to finish work started.

The last petitioner had left the boss's office. Paul stretched his arms high and took a deep breath. Was all forgotten? No! There was a knock at the door. Paul, somewhat irritated shouted „Yes", and Rita walked in. Paul thought okay! Rita seemed to be very aroused and her cheeks were quite red.

„Rita, why are you here after working hours? Is something wrong in your department?"

Although at first confused by the unawaited question, then it all came bubbling out.

„Uh, what? No, no everything's OK. But, can't you see it?"

Paul saw nothing, instead of which he looked cluelessly at Rita.

„What am I supposed to see?"

„Me, you still remember the Christmas party."

Paul: „here we go."

„Afterwards. It was really hot!! I haven't spoken to anyone

about it."

Paul: relieved to hear that.

„But now, everyone is asking:"Rita what happened? Your skin rash? It's almost disappeared? What did you do?"

Paul: sounds like an aftermath.

„Look at me Herr Wieland. Isn't my skin much better?"

Unwillingly Paul did as he was told. Then his lips stuttered out the dull question: „So what?"

„Boss, you have to help me. You can't just leave me half way there." Rita was on fire. It was like Schiller's „Don Carlos" where Posa the idealist threw out his demands at King Phillip II:

„Sire, we want freedom of thought!"

Admittedly, Rita's sounded a bit more banal:

„Boss, let me give you another blowjob!"

The effect was the same to Phillip and Paul, they were dumbfounded and had to think about it.

„What do you think this is?" Asked Phillip, no, it was Paul. There was no stopping Rita now.

„Boss I've found out that you don't have a girlfriend at the moment, so I thought, doing it „French" is better than jerking off!"

Rita was shocked at her own audacity.

„Frau Göhler, are you serious? I think you're going too far!"

„Boss, put yourself in my position. Here I am walking around with a spotty face and can't find a man. And then this miracle happens. You have to help me."

„I don't have to do anything! I think it best if we part ways. I'll terminate your contract."

Rita's reaction was icy and angry.

„Boss, I wouldn't do that if I was you, because then the co-workers and the customers will all find out why!"

Paul's inner voice told him: „Draw in your horns and don't go too far."

Paul managed to get the situation under control again. And, in a very business-like manner, they came to an agreement. It must be after business hours. Rita should pretend to work on some flawed brassiere, while Paul checked the order book until everyone had left the building, but for the cleaning ladies who always began by cleaning the production rooms and would only get to his office an hour later. The opportunity was here, Paul felt that he was very turned on, as his thoughts wandered down to his dick and the first signs of physical change in his penis were visible. Rita appeared not to have noticed. And then it was time. Rita appeared wearing a coat. Paul should have known that she wouldn't be wearing a negligee? In one hand she had a small bottle of egg-liqueur and in the other two glasses.

„Boss, you're so shy!"

She laughed naughtily and pointed at the glasses.

„This just has to be."

Then, both slurped the stuff down. Both had to laugh heartily and Paul felt relieved. Before Paul could invite her, she was down on her knees skillfully unzipping his pants and with her right hand gently pulled out his penis, and with a few ups and downs, the little man was ready to go, and quick as a whip he disappeared down the cavern of her throat. Unfortunately for Paul, the sexual act seemed much too short. After a few moments he felt the first flashes in his limbs and the right side of his brain lit up, followed by an „Aiiiiii!"

„Oh God, oh God, oh God" and to Paul's disappointment it was all over.

Rita did a great job: the last drop was sucked out of Paul, then the fly was zipped up in a quick movement. Rita looked up at Paul from her petitioner's position and whispered:

„One more time?"

Whether Paul agreed through a straight answer or just a nod of the head, is not clear. At least he didn't say „No!" A deep „thank you very much" and Rita was gone. All of a sudden Paul felt quite naked and weak-kneed.

4

„Hello Shark“

„Hello Paul, how are you?“

„Hard to say. So far I haven't been able to visualise this in my dirtiest fantasies!“

And while Paul reported forcefully and in detail, Sharks senastions caused a discrete swelling in his pants.

„Paul, you'll be lucky if your adventure doesn't get spread around. Take note of the juiciest parts of it and you'll have a hot story for your erotic calender.“

I've taken note of it and now I'm ready to take over a James Bond role.“

„Don't get carried away. Have you checked how many girls with bad skins work for you?“

„No, why?“

„Because you could establish a special sanatorium in your company. Then you will be doubly needed and thoroughly sucked out.“

„That is the fate of the merciful! I'm sure all the healed women will remain as thankful employees.“

„But your job remains dangerous and your salary modest. Actually, you deserve better!“

5

Work left neither Paul nor Rita much time for adventurous thoughts or actions. Business was flourishing. This made Paul strong. His self-confidence grew, his appearance more forceful and there were less „ifs" and „buts". During his everyday checks in the company, Paul was able to determine that Rita's spots and warts had, after their little contact, indeed disappeared. Rita now had a tasty face you could nibble on! She had also undergone quite a change. She had a positive approach to life, was optimistic, laughing and glowing from within. Everyone marvelled at Rita.

The story could have ended here. But, it didn't, because, Rita had the *helper syndrome*!

About three weeks later she appeared with Carmen Wittchen, a new employee, in her boss's office. She was all excited again. This time with Carmen in tow, and one could understand how embarrased Carmen was through Rita's words of explanation.

„Boss, we're here alone and no one can hear us. Carmen is my best friend, and she has just got a job with us. And, Herr Wieland, take a look at her, she has acne, just like I used to have. So, as I still have a favour open from you, I thought to myself „Rita you're pretty enough now, give your friend Carmen the gift of the treatment instead!"

It took Paul quite a time to digest this chunk of information.

Trying to comprehend Rita's logic caused his lungs to gasp for air and his brain to search for evidence. His anger grew through this flood of information. Rita noticed just in time.

„Boss, calm down, nothing has changed."

„Hold on." Paul burst out: „Do you think I have nothing better to do than hang my dick out for the whole staff?

„Of course not!" Rita, trying to reassure him. „Couldn't you do it with Carmen in her lunch break?"

Now the first breach of trust in Paul and Rita's aqauintance raised it's head. Rita led the petit Carmen behind Paul's desk. It was an older model, where the interconnection made it impossible for the visitor to see the legs opposite one. Rita nodded at Carmen and before Paul knew what was happening, Carmen was down on her knees. Paul was perplexed. There was nothing standing in the way of Paul's volcanic eruption now. Then there was a knock on the door and before Paul could say a word, a customer-friend walked into the office.

„Hello Paul."

„Hello Walter."

The usual greetings ceremonial.

„Paul, excuse me, but I was passing by and am just popping in to see you.. It's about the promotion in four weeks. I need additional goods, you'll have no problem with."

This seemed the right moment to get out of Paul's sight. However, she forgot to take Carmen, who was hiding under Paul's desk between his pants legs. Coffee and sandwiches were brought in and a lively conversation began.

„The consignment is almost complete, if we get stuck in, we might even be able to deliver fourteen days earlier."

Paul's voice faltered. Carmen seems to have misunderstood. All of a sudden Paul felt Carmen's hands on his fly. She wouldn't...would she? Oh yes she would! Her determined hands invaded his trousers, finding the opening to his slip and even more determinedly grabbed his penis, which instantly reacted positively and enormously. Paul winced.

„Is something wrong Paul?"

„No, no, just a little overworked, so to say pumped dry."

„I can well imagine, as if everything was hitting into you from above and below."

„Not just into!"

„I felt the same when my Dad passed away 4 years ago. One grows into it."

Paul could confrim that. His penis no longer fitted in his pants. Carmen did the only right thing to do. She took the growing giant out with both hands.

„I'm sure you'll make your way. Don't let those old workers of your father's get you down."

„Mother."

„I'm happy for you, everything looks just fine." Carmen nodded from under the desk.

„And don't overdo things! That can happen when one hasn't been in the „metier" for long."

Nothing helped. Carmen swallowed Paul's whole cock right to the hairy balls. Now the colleague down below really got to work.

„You know, I really don't like the look of you. Shall I get you a glass of water?"

„No thanks, it'll pass."

„Well I think it's getting worse."

„Yes, it always takes a little time to get used to new circumstances."

Carmen was moving in on her target. To distract, a desperate Paul told a dirty „man-joke". His ejaculation hit right at the punch-line. Walter was a bit confused at the way Paul was telling the story, which included eye rolling and body twitching. Now that the joke was over, everyone seemed to relax.

„Paul, I'm going to get you a glass of water."

„You know what Walter, you go ahead to dispatch. I'll meet you there."

Once again Walter was confused by Paul's behaviour. But it would all work itself out. No sooner had Walter left the room, than Paul jumped up out of his chair. Nothing to fear. His pants were zipped up. Everything clean. Carmen had come prepared by Rita. Before Paul could start shouting, Carmen calmed him down:

„Boss, everything went well. Your customer is waiting. I'll disappear. Careful!, that no one sees me."

Carmen behaved just like Rita's shadow.

6

„Shark! Old buddy!"

„Paul! Old Sucker! Come on, tell Uncle Doctor what happened to the good, innocent little boy Paul. Everything that happened."

And Paul started bubbling over like a radio reporter. Meticulously but oh so sensationalistically too.

„On the one hand, it's a very simple urban erotic story, the likes of which you'll find thousands of in our society. On the other hand, a criminal misdemeanour, should someone press charges. That could cost a lot of cash."

„My head is spinning. I have to keep cool!"

„Have you checked, to see how many girls with bad skin work for you?"

„Yes, seven."

„The you're really going to be sucked dry."

„It's easy for you to talk. What should I do?"

„I see two options. You either stop it, by telling them that you've contracted some venereal disease, or you make a business out of it?"

„How?"

„That, I still have to work out. How do you turn an action into an attraction?"

Paul was living dangerously. Jealous people, who you can find in any firm, could find out about his carryings on and put him in an embarrasing situation. How should he behave? What should he do? Paul was amazed at how everything was taking it's course, covered in a blanket of silence. Rita seemed to be the „Godmother" of a secret sect of bad skinned women, all discrete and conspiratorial.She saw to it that Paul wasn't over-exerted. She arranged the time and place. She also noticed that Paul's penis was developing wonderfully and growning larger. At the same time she regretted to see that a longer time was needed, to come to ejaculation. Could it have been compassion or affection: Rita often put a little refreshment on his desk and sometimes even a flower. Paul spoke to Rita.

„Rita, you are my Lamprey."

„Lamprey? What's that?"

„The Lamprey is a serpentine fish!"

One should now know that Paul was an Ichtyologue. Even as a kid, he used his pocket money to buy an aquarium and breed sticklebacks. Later, Paul changed to tropical fish and read any literature on fish that he could get hold of. But then, work ate him up and he had no time for fish, instead he now and again ate fish.

„Am I as cold as a fish?"

Rita smiled mischievously.

„No, but tempramentally a fish; they're the hotest lovers!"

„What about the snake-like Lamprey, that's supposed to be like me?"

„The Lamprey is a scavenger. He lurks on the bottom near the shore, when a stately fish swims by overhead, he shoots up attaching himself to the underbelly. And then he begins to suck and to suck."

„The poor attacked fish! Does he get sucked out? And must he die?"

„Generally not. Once the Lamprey has stuffed itself, it breaks away from the host. It still has to procreate. But, there's something else! It doesn't take long for other scavengers to be lured. And many hounds hunt the hare."

Rita seemed to be very caring.

„Is it getting too much for you?" Paul nodded.

Rita reduced it to three time a week. Paul mainly distributed his sperm drung the breaks or after hours, wherever possible: in his office under the desk, in the warehouse, his executive toilet, the lumber room, in the heater or even in his car.

„Shark, it can't go on like this."

„Chin up Paul! When the Paulian *Fresh-Juice-Therapy* kicks in, your clientel can be released, all healthy and cured."

„You won't believe it. The therapy is working! Rashes on face, back, thighs, and anywhere else, are no longer to be seen. The success of the cure is daunting."

„So, why do they continue sucking?"

„I suspect that they're my co-workers friends. Whenever I ask, they tell me that they are temporary employees, in which case I can't be bothered to check."

„You should. Paul, you're being taken advatage of."

„With everyone hanging on your cock, you should be making a profit. And, they really get cured?"

„Really!"

„Paul, I'm beginning to get an idea."

„That's scary!"

„Doesn't have to be. For now, it's just a conceptual attempt. I must admit that , up until now I thought it was a fantasy, wishfull thinking. Now I'm getting a little curious. It's heading toward reality. I need a test. At the end of the day, I'm a pharmacist. In my pharmacy I hear all the devastating complaints about dermatologists. Of all doctors, they have the lowest success rate. They prescribe balms and creams and even more balms, but hardly any help." After a short pause he continues.

„I have a small furnished flat in the city, that is not being rented at the moment."

„That's great. Is it your hideaway, you old bugger?"

„You're right. Now you know why my wife left me. But, that's all in the past. Now we can try our trial run there."

„What if I've had enough?"

„I have something fantastic planned."

„What do I say to the girls?"

„Tell them that you've caught some venereal disease and need some time to recuperate. Then we can test our experiment."

„I want to quit now, and here you come with the continuation."

„Just do me this one favour Paul. You owe it to me. Remember Marianne!"

„You're mean to remind me of her now. But, I admit, you saved me from that fury."

„I'll prepare everything for the test and we should be ready in fourteen days."

„And how long should the test last?"

„I hope that within three months we'll know whether or not to prolong for the same period of time."

„Paul, that's enough for today. I need time to think about this!"

„I think it's going to be great."

9

Did Paul do as his friend Shark had told him? At any rate he took his friend's advice and, putting on a sad face, told his petitioners about his venereal disease, without going into detail. Generous as Paul was, he allowed a few „after-treatments" (at their own risk), but did not take on any new patients. Instead of which he concentrated more on his underwear company. Business had become harder. Imports were pressuring the German market.

Shark called, the apartment was ready for action and they only needed to check it again to see if anything was missing.

Paul was surprised. The apartment was in the centre of town, but the entrance, although clean and decent, did not attract attention as it was on the side of the building facing the neighbouring plot. A real hideaway. It consisted of one larger room, the practice, two smaller adjacent rooms, a little bathroom and a small kitchen. The walls of the rooms were painted white, and the floors were also tiled in white. So, it was all clean and tidy. The interior decoration, spartanically simple. A lounger, or was it a nursing bed? To be adjusted up or down. The smaller rooms were furnished with tables and chairs. Finally, a stove, a dishwasher and even a dryer completed the establishment.

„Is it worth all this effort?"

„Don't worry, I can rent the apartment as it is as a small practice."

Paul had no reason to complain. Shark was in a hurry. He gave Paul the key and left the apartment. Paul stood there for a while longer, lost in thought in his new workplace.

„Am I crazy? What am I getting into?"

His arguments soothed him: it was just on the side, and so far his health hadn't suffered and his dick had grown more impressive and stable. The advantages were obvious! He just had to reduce the effort! There was still the company! It was going well, be it with great input.

Pleased with himself, Paul locked the door and left his new place of employment.

10

„Hello Paul! Shark here!"

„Yes, Shark?"

„We can start. I've also bought towels, kitchen rolls, soap etc. and taken them to the institute."

„I'd love to hepl Shark. I was passing our spot the other day and saw that you had put up a sign. Not bad, very subtle!"

„How did you come up with „Studio Paul Pensano"?"

„Oh, I had a whole bunch of ideas: for example, „Shagging Shack", „Cock spot" „Horny Giant Inn", „Paul and Shark", but that one was taken, finally Paul Pensano; Pen stands for penis and Sano means I heal!"

Paul had to laugh.

„By the way, I've had small business cards printed."

„Shark, you're crazy! How far do you want to take this? We were talking about testing for a quarter of a year."

„No stress, don't worry, it is just a test, but we have to conduct it under real condtions. I have so many ideas!"

„Oh God, oh God!"

„By the way, I've also arranged the first appointment."

„Oh God!"

„No, it's not him!"

„We agreed. Only on weekends, Sundays and holidays?"

„Exactly. It's on 6th February, a Saturday at 3pm."

„Who is she, or rather what is she like?"

„Old and ugly and defaced by seborrhoae."
„Oh God, oh God!"

11

The first day under Shark's direction arrived. During the time before this, Paul had been imagining the worst scenarios and all that could go wrong. He spoke to Rita, informing her of what was happening and asked her if she would become his assistant. Rita promptly and happily agreed to. Paul negotiated a good hourly rate for Rita. Rita agreed to everything. So, she really could always rely on her boss. Apart from this her behaviour was like the motto „It's being a part of it that matters!" She was simply curious by nature!

Paul arrived at the site two hours early. Rita was already waiting at the door. They went in very excited. First, they turned up the heat to make sure that the rooms were nice and warm. Rita had brought her portable radio with her.

„Please put it in the side room and play some soft music! Did you also bring a player? Good, I brought Ravel's „Bolero" to be played when the action starts, not before!"

„I think I need a tranquilizer."

„No you can't do that. The dick must get stiff, if it doesn't grow, then everything was for nothing!"

„Viagra?"

„I wouldn't advise that, all you have to do is have an ejaculation. Don't be worried. I am here."

„Thank God, what luck!"

„I'll make you another cup of tea!"

„Everything, as promised:

„I'll put on the nurse's costume now and receive the lady, by the way, her name is Maierwild, explain evrything to her, how it works, then bring her to you in the practice, all clear?"

„Oh God, oh God!"

She didn't look anything like Shark's warning. A little over forty and somewhat chubby, but really very friendly. Unlike Paul, she was not at all nervous.

Rita handed Paul a note which read: „Pump the healing syrup, using the handpump with your own hands, swallow immediately, while still at body temperature. Coffe or a digestive of your choice!"

Armed with this information, Paul lay down on the lounger wearing his bathrobe.Rita raised the lounger. Frau Maierwild sat diectly next to him watching with interest.

Rita opened the bathrobe. What Frau maierwild saw was good and grown but not really encouraging. She looked surprised, then laughed and asked Paul.

„Nervous? Am I the first?"

Paul nodded vigorously and turning to Rita:

„The Bolero please!"

Frau Maierwild on the other hand was quite practical.

„Well then, let's get started."

Then, with an experienced grip she got hold of Paul's cock, and with the rythmic moving up and down the Bolero sent it's message and immediately the little animal started to grow.

„See!"

Was the positive comment to the developement, and the cock kept growing

„Oh" said Fau Maierwild and then a bit later another"Oh".

Paul's cock was now standing upright showing a remarkable size. She paused:

„May I change the prescription?"

Paul nodded, and in a rapid move, Frau Maierwild was up and devoured Paul's whole penis. Where did it go? It completely disappeared into her head. Had it shrunk? No, it had grown even larger. The Eternal Creator had endowed Frau Maierwild with an anatomy that only a sword swallower in the circus could boast of. They were both having a tremendously great time, which Rita noticed with a slightly saturnine look.

So what! Paul cried out loud, and then again and again. Rita gave Frau maierwild a shove.

„Stop it, stop it!"

Frau Maierwild finally let go and Paul groaned his:

"Oh God oh God!"

They were all happy now, even Rita after getting a good tip.

„I'll organise an appointment with Herr Shark, as he's the one I have to settle up with."

Paul wanted to know more, but Frau Maierwild was already at the door. She turned around one more time and said:

„That was a delicious dick."

Rita treated Paul just like a child, his cock carefully cleaned off with a damp cloth and then gave him a cup of coffee. Paul was tired now. Let's let him sleep here at the scene of his first triumph.

12

„Shark?"

„Yes, Paul? So, how did it go?"

„After the first nervousness, it went well for both sides. Everyone got what they wanted. Frau Maierwild is an anatomical wonder! My whole pride and joy disappeared down her throat!"

„But, the feedback was quite „reasonable", maybe she left a little wrinkled manniken behind, but your little sack is filled with ducats."

„Shark, we haven't spoken about that at all. What are the costs? Do you charge a fee?

„I've worked out the following package. An advance of 50 Euros for the rent plus utilities for each treatment. I only require a fee after a successful treatment., at least when it is visibly so."

„This form of accounting is totally strange to me, I'm dumbfounded!"

„We'll think about it all after the test run.""Do you have another client?"

„What do you mean „one"? There is already a reservation list ."

„Unbelievable! And it all remains anonymous?"

„Trust me. By the way. I've had inquiries from men! May I accept them?"

„Shark! No way! I, or should I say „he" , is only turned on by women. There's no way I would get a „hard on" for a man, not to speak of spurting sperm.

„What a pity that we have to do without this target group. But, the resonance in the ladies field is quite sufficent.Paul, your next appointment is on Sunday 14th. February. After that I would like to increase to two and then three times a week."

13

They arrived in the practice as a pair. Frau Künzli from Stuttgart with her niece. Unfortunately only Frau Künzli wanted to be treated. Paul murmured: „Is this going to work?"

He had enough grounds for this prognosis. Frau Künstli had already overstepped the fifty year mark, with a sharply angular cut face, a pointed nose, glasses and dyed curls. That's what made up Frau Künstli.

„Amazing everyzing zatt can happen" she babbled.

„I have been like ziss for sirty years and now I hear zer iss zis man out zere. So Vhat are ve vaiting for?"

The note said the same as it had with Frau Maierwild, pump the healing syrup using the handpump with your own hands ... etc. etc. Paul looked at Frau Künstli's hands; scrawny, wrinkled and bony! This could be fun.

Frau Künstli got to work with Swabian vigour.She was a hard worker. After ten minutes and the Bolero being played for the third time. Nothing! Or to be more precise, hardly anything!

„Vhat is zhiss? Here I am already working for half an hour and I am getting Sirsty! But I don't get nussing!"

Frau Künstli was an experienced woman and she remained friendly. Rita entered, and seeing the look on Paul's face, made a baffling suggestion to the helpless two.

„Frau Künstli, didn't you come with someone else? Should we get her involved as well?"

Frau Künstli was a bit surprised.

„If you sink so. She can drive a car, so, my girl Edithle can surely use her hands!"

She came into the operating room. She was young, had a classy figure and immediately sized up the situation.

„I'll be happy to do it for you!"

And, just like her aunty, she grabbed Paul's dick with swabian intensity and began massaging it with both hands. Naturally, it grew.Paul already had drops of sweat on his forehead. His tool looked demolished with blue pressure marks. Edithle paused.

„May I try another method Aunty?"

„Knock yourself out!"

To everyone's amazement, Edithle sat down on Paul's lap. Her experienced hands slipped under her skirt and everyone knew what she was about to do. Paul's penis had hardly entered Edithle's tender abdomen, when she started to swing her hips rythmically, elaborating with:

„Hey, hey, I'm a showjumper, this is how I do it."

A little while later:

„Vhere iss ze glass?"

Edithle managed everything that afternoon. Aunty Künstle got her cocktail.

„Zhiss doesn't taste bad at all, it actually tastes gut, like nut liquer!"

Edithle wanted to try some too. She also received a few drops, so everyone left happy and satisfied.

„You're a Son of a Bitch!"

„Paul?"

„You knew that Swabian trainwreck! You shouldn't have done this to me!"

„It all went well. It was worth it. And isn't she attractive?"

„Swabian! With iron hands! My penis still hurts today. Even the Bolero was too short, we had to repeat the Coda again when the rider jumped on me."

„A quick tour de force. Calm down Paul, that brought in a lot. It was for two!"

„Hold on! I don't even know how much you take in. Are our costs at least covered?"

„You can say that again!The first trial period has just ended. If we check our balance, during this period you have treated 32 patients. 23 have already paid the Cure Premium.

Our expenses were:

Rent 800 x 3 plus 25% utilities

Rita 64 hours x 20

Commission, agency fees

„Hold on, hold on! I hear commission, do you charge something for that?"

„I do 15%"

„What's left then? Do we at least cover costs?"

„As you can see?"

„Oh, God!"

That's €23.800 for you. If you continue working like this it will be € 95.200 for this year. My commission already deducted."

Paul had to pause for a second, he was speechless.

„Oh God!"

„Hello Paul, you okay? Hung up. You'll need to digest this one!"

„Boatsman, now you touch the nipple with your lips, it's a galleon's breast; moisten it with your tongue and suck gently, not like a hungry baby, but rather hot and delicate. Circle our tongue clockwise around the nipple. Let your fingers take over. Finally, even you will notice how the nipple erects, just like a penis. How about the other side. Time to change sides."

„Aye, aye Sir."

„We've got time. There's a mellow breeze. The captain is breathing heavily. With the captain's permission, you may carefully massage Rita's luscious breasts. Then off to the stern (*rear*). To the legs. Which is the most delicate part? The inner, upper thigh! Bare that in mind Boatsman."

„Above the right knee, that's where we begin with the finger. It's like the beginning of the „*Freischütz*" overture, right out of the blue;when does one hear the first sound? But, then it's there, softly at first, keep it piano. Upwards, a little louder, then down again, a little less, but increasingly higher. Yes, right up to the Gates of Paradise. The Gates are still closed for you. Stop, da capo, back to the beginning, but this time moisten it with your tongue. You feel the sea coming alive."

„Yes, and now to the starboard, the crew has to go all out.

Now we get to the dungeon's dance, around the Golden Fleece. Let's hope the ship remains on calm seas and doesn't get lost in the tangle of Saragossa!"

"All focus is on the centre, moving in a circle from hip to vagina and da capo, da capo amid the immense trembling of the hull, rising and sinking in the swell of the waves. The boatsman stays calm. Driving into Paradise with his middle finger, which is the longest. No, still not there, The vulva wants to be greeted and stroked. It begins to swell. Filled with blood. What do you have lips and a tongue for? Boatsman do your duty."

"And now, in the upward swing of the rump, you drive in deeper, and if not moist, there's a "can" in the galley so you can! Massage the moisture all the more. There behind the vulva you come upon a nobble. A woman's clitoris, not quite as massive as a man's penis, but just as sensitive. Handle it gently, yes, with the tongue as well. Take your time. Your journey's not over yet. Half a mile above is the G-Point. An intensive feminine membrane, linger there, caressing. "As an ace you bet, you will soon be wet", be it at the moment of orgasm, the super-pleasure. Now it's up to you to decide, to stay on course until orgasm, or to steer your warmed up Love-motor with full speed ahead into the Harbour of Love."

It was hard not to drive the game onward. He could feel Rita's willingness. But there was still the pilot. The captain lay prone, unable to move on the bed.

Unsatisfied and grumpy,Paul got up and went into the bathroom for a cold shower. Marlisa managed in the shortest time, with Rita's approval to successfully bring Paul's work to a head. Rita sank back on the deck. Paul thought about money.

In the end , all three agreed to continue the tuition.

„As you can see."

„Oh God!"

„That's 23.800€ for you. If you keep working at this rate it'll be 95.200€ this year, and that's after deducting my commission."

„Paul held his breath for a minute. He was speechless."

„Oh God!"

„Hello Paul, are you okay? Hung up. Looks like he'll have to digest this first."

15

„Oh God", Paul was still mumbling the next day. He hadn't expected anything like this. He started to get doubtful. His side job was providing a higher income than his job in the company. The situation there had worsened. Some of the best clients having left, the big ones being eaten up by large corporations, the smaller ones having to close up shop! Is this how it was going to carry on? No, it didn't look good, and that had him worried.

Paul worked longer in the company, it was just the „Trade Fairs" that he visited on some Saturdays or Sundays. No one knew why? His new hobby, on the other hand, made even more fun, especially now that he knew how much he was making! Not only did it bring in more money, but it also changed his equipment. His penis, grew not only more and more in dimension, but took on a classical form, or at least that is what he thought. His observations showed the following: By hand his penis got longer but decreased in volume. Orally, it got more volumnous, which Paul preferred. This brought to mind an old saying: „Long and slim, for girls too thin. Short and thick does the trick!"

Be careful Paul? For how long can you do the job? It could well go on up until retirement, but how highly concentrated would the „load" be then? So, there were also problems there! But not as big! He took on the next assignment with a certain sense of ease. A neat, petit, athletic girl entered the consulting room.

„How old are you, if you don't mind my asking?"

„22 years old.",

„Please excuse my curiosity,but I don't see any rash on you."

„Our patient is waiting in the next room."

The girl explained smilingly. Rita who had entered the room nodded. To his surprise, Paul soon realised how versed the girl was in doing what she was doing. No sooner had Paul opened his gown and Rita turned on the „Bolero", then she was on him, with both her hands twirling his dick and softly touching his foreskin, so that with no effort Paul's „Little man" grew and grew. A short"may I?" and a nod from Paul and her lips, tongue and mouth and whatever brought her nearer her goal: the orgasm and the flow of semen. This was dutifully collected as ordered and taken into the next room.

„That was wonderful!"

Paul burst out enthusiastically.

„And so gentle. You can come again."

The girl thanked him politely. A little later as she came out of the toilet, Paul stopped his visitor for a second.

„Just one more question! Who taught you this art?" She replied with a sweet smile.

„Our patient sitting in the waiting room, my uncle."

16

„Shark, you really got me there!"

„Well, it didn't do any harm."

„No, but with a man? I would have failed."

„Don't underestimate the Gays! They can be as tender as a woman. But, now for something else. We've reached the second test phase. I just need a few more visits and then we're done!"

„I don't get it, done with what?"

„Done with testing the main skin irritations. That should do it!"

„What did we test?"

„We tested how successful the treatment was to the most common skin ailments."

„And what were they?"

„Acne. Occurs mainly in younger people with a mis-balanced hormone household. They have spots, pustules and papules on face and cleavage."

„Keep it short Shark!"

„There are, Psoriasis, Rosacea, Atopic Eczema, Herpes, Warts,......."

„Stop I'm already itching all over in possible and impossible parts of my body!"

„To put it in a nutshell. All test patients immediately got rid of their Acne. The treatment for Psoriasis is more complicated.“

„Are those the large dry flakes of skin?“

„That‘s it. Inflamed areas of skin as large as a plate. All in all, a difficult disease to cure.“

„And, can we cure it?“

„Yes, you can.“

„Thanks for the compliment!“

„Imagine it, your juice only failed in one of twelve cases. That‘s a sensational success quota of 91.7%. That is how we‘ll establish our reputation.“

„Can you stop your briefing now?“

„Okay, for now. Let‘s talk about someting nice. Let‘s talk about vacation. Question: when does your Bra Company take vacation?“

„Just like every year, we take our vacation in May, late spring. Why do you ask?“

„In those three weeks we can expand our practice. We have the means. We just need to invest more time and effort. Do you agree?“

„And how! I have a few wishes.“

„I‘m taking notes....“

A few minutes later. „That‘s enough. It‘s about time you stopped.“

It‘s good that our pharmacist enjoyed an intense and comprehnesive education at university. He didn‘t necessarily need all this knowledge behind the counter. Now he had a real challenge. And he was really enjoying this.

17

Paul recuperated splendidly on the Algarve. Really pretty women, most of them attractive, strolled by „to and fro" right before his wide open eyes. And then just the opposite „fro and to". They wondered why this good looking young man showed no reaction to their flirting. Was he ill? To be honest, at a closer look, he seemed a little sucked dry! Was he gay? Then at least some of his lovers should show up in the eighteen days they were there. So, Paul remained a mystery to the „women's world" on the coast of Portugal. The women soon discovered with admiration that Paul's bathing trunks were getting tighter, but before any turmoil could break out Paul had to get on back home.

Filled with pride, Shark presented the refurbished practice to the homecomer.

There was a huge lounger right in the middle.

„Is this the seat for a luxury dental treatment? One side is free, so that your patient will be able to reach your „healing fountain" easily. It's very comfortable to lie on and look: you can change the seat into any position."

So, Shark started pushing buttons that would leave Paul in the weirdest positions.

Shark had indeed fulfilled all his wishes; the reception and waiting rooms were very modern and the consulting room was even more up to date. Sharks superfluous paintings had finally found the perfect spot.

The show could go on. Rita was also bursting with revitalised energy. She had to deal with the next patient first. The patient was a teacher, a professor at a language oriented high school. Teachers are hard to handle, unlike their students, they question everything like there's no tomorrow.

„Isn't it possible to send the little bottle of sperm - how many millilitres are even in there - by post?"

„No, the sooner this medicine gets from creator to patient, the more powerful it's effect."

„How about the hygiene in this institute?"

„It's the optimum! Look at the bathroom, it's like a laboratory. I thoroughly clean Mr Paulonius' private parts twice before each treatment."

„Really? Thoroughly?"

„Oh yes, sometimes too thoroughly. We sometimes even lose the precious sperm through an ejaculation! I've had my experiences!"

„Do you at least clean him up with a disinfectant?"

„Only after the „act". If an atom of disinfectant were to touch the penis before the treatment, it would radically reduce the cure."

„Who can guarantee that Mr. Paulonius can donate sufficient sperm? Theoretically, one should measure the ejection before taking it."

„That would prolong the way immensely and thus weaken the impact. We've just spoken about this! We measured the normal quantity, which is on an average 140 mg. Anyway, you're not paying for the amount, but rather the effectiveness.

We only charge for the visible success."

At any rate, Rita's explanation seemed to finally be sufficient. Once our teacher took action, she droppped all reservations and went straight for it. She'd never seen such great big beautiful dick before, let alone suck on it. So, it was no big surprise that her activities caused her to have a wild orgasm herself, which opened up the question as to whether this could be considered a customer service to be introduced into the programme? Paul handled this delay masterfully, without plunging into a premature orgasm himself. The „Bolero" was started up again in the middle, while the aroused teacher called out:

„Not so bad at all! Really good! Keep it up! Shall we do it again?"

„Not today, visit us again soon!"

18

„Shark, old chap! Paul here. Sometimes I've just about had enough. My tongue hanging out of my mouth and my dick out of my pants!"

„Paul just close up the openings and keep your tools where they belong. So, tell me what's wrong with you?"

„I have a problem. Lately, the „handjobs" seem to be on the increase."

„That's because of your older clients! They want nothing to do with your „masterpiece". But, that also has it's advantages."

„That may be so, but my penis is getting longer and slimmer. Soon I'll be able to wrap it around me."

„Well, then we'll just have to come up with an alternative."

„I've been thinking about it."

„Me too! I'm sure that what can be used for milking cows, sheep and goats, can be used for something else too."

„That's enough thank you! You jerk, I mean those suction pumps that are used for breast feeding mothers."

„Of course! Yes, naturally! But doesn't that just suck out the extra pressure in the mother's breast? Can you keep up with that? Apart from that, won't the sucker have to be adjusted to your penis."

„Do you think it'll work?"

„That'll be an expensive gadget."

„And what if it doesn't work?"

„Then we'll donate it to the anthrolopological museum in Dingelfingen. The whole damned machine, including a print of your previuosly great „masterpiece!"

„Jealosy is an ugly trait."

19

Paul looked up. He caught his breath! He sat there motionless and speechless. So, the new patient reacted instead.

„Hello Paul."

„Hello Marlisa."

Then after a while: „I wasn't expecting this."

„I wanted to surprise you, but maybe it wasn't the right thing to do."

A weak voiced Paul replied.

„Well, it sure worked."

„Come on Paul, try to look just a little bit pleased."

„Why do we especially have to meet here? I have to admit, the situaton is a bit embarrasing. How did you find me?"

„Through Shark. I walked into a pharmacy in our little town and there was Shark. We chatted about old times at high school and we spoke about you! It was very inspiring. He is still your friend. Then he made a suggestion. Why not visit Paul! So, here I am. Come on Paul, stop pulling such a stupid face. I'm so glad to see you again." Marlisa knew how to smooth Paul's ruffled feathers and then he was able to enjoy the conversation. The mood lifted and they were both relaxed. They sat down at a table and their memories brought the first laughter. As arranged, Rita arrived with the champagne. Two glasses were poured and two candles lit as it was already twilight outside. Rita hung the „closed" sign on the door before preparing a small snack of delicacies for the pair and then discretely left them.

Marlisa and Paul had a lot to talk about. Had they been lovers? Yes and no. Emotionally they had reached the intensity of Romeo and Juliet, but the physical intimacy was lacking. So it was that during her studies Marlisa met the German director of a factory in Brazil, whom she eventually married. But, the passion was soon gone. Was it the work, the boring social life in San Paolo, or the childlessness? Her husband's early death, falling off a horse, saved them from a divorce. Now she had his fortune and her freedom. Her girlfriends all envied her! She wanted to go back to Germany to see her old chaste friend again.

„Pauly, I loved you more than anything.“

„But „wham bam“, you left me just like that.“

„Today we can talk about it, especially now that I know what you're up to! Pauly, you were too well nurtured. Your mother, was like Cerberus watching your every step. And, once I dared to touch your pants. To stroke what was underneath. He got wet, you got embarrased and ran away. So, I said to myself, Marlisa this is no fun and it has no future.“

Now they could have a good laugh at it, but it was in deadly ernest back then.

And while they were laughing: „Seeing your developement today gets me all hot and bothered.“

Paul whispered: „Then, come and see for yourself.“

With a „yes“, Marlisa's hand unbuttoned his pants, her hand searching for the opening of his slip. Shocked, she whispered.

„This is awful!“

After a while, „great!“ And her expedition continued.

The underpants got too tight, the pants as well.

„What have you been up to Pauly?"

While her left hand held onto Paul's dick, her right hand either brought the champagne glass to her mouth, or stroked his body wherever uncovered. He drank from her mouth, where, between the cool drinking, hot passionate kisses aroused their desire.

Hot and cold. Wet and dry. They were living out their lust.

Finally Paul spoke: „Please,"

They both got up, as if in a trance, and without loss of any tenderness they swayed out of the room.

In the next room, which was only softly lit, they turned the large lounger, staging it into their battlefield of love. Marlisa took command. After removing all profanities from her body, her passion took over! How could setting up the troops be so erotic and exciting!

Now the inevitable came to pass. The troops were ready. Both sides totally naked spraying one another with champagne, too wet. Time to suck it all up, kissing every square centimetre. At first contact Marlisa drove her flanks into battle, and pressed her opponents campagne wet cannon with a grenadiers grip onto her ballwark-vagina. Paul's bayonette was caught. He resisted, quietly hissing. Paul set his troops in motion. The situation was serious. Battlesounds arose. Attack! Hissing and moaning and driving on to „hiss-moaning." Stop! Pauly's troops must move in to attack. By manouvering the cavallery with a sideways swing, he turned the tide of battle. With a thrust and a swing, Marlisie's infantry was tied down. And Sir Paul thrust to, mercilessly with his lance. Thrust by thrust, the revenge for all previous love's abstinence. Marlisa whimpered, let her, she began to scream. Let her. Screams of passion.

Not enough: once loaded, our well trained Paul pulled his merser out of this position, aiming it at Marlisie's backside, and a bacchanal drumroll began. With a lusty scream Paul rammed his cannon into Marlisa's ammuntion store. In surrender she stretched her backside high, but Paul's warrior was in the fever of passion: with a hurrah, ,hurrah, he kept ramming it into poor Marlisie, heading for an orgasm. How many had Marlisa had?

They turned on their sides laughing happily and holding each other tightly. They had both won the battle, carrýing the victory together.

„Spooning", they drifted off into sleep.

20

„Hello Shark."

„Hello Paul. How are you? How well did you survive the encounter? Something you weren't expecting, right?"

„You arranged that very well. But, please not too often."

„But Paul, wasn't that a remarkable moment in your life?"

„Yes."

„You're not very talkative today. Did something go wrong?"

„No, I'll tell you later. But, can you imagine it, I have got an offer to sell."

„You don't want to sell our business, do you?"

„No, I'm talking about my company."

„Your lingerie factory?"

„Yes. A foreign company wants to buy it. The information is excellent."

„Paul, I can only advise you to do it."

„I have a bad concience. It all started so well. But, the market has changed. The buyers aren't even interested in the manufacturing, all they care about is the brand name and my customers."

„Paul, do it."

„Imagine. Thirty years ago my parents bought a small tailor's shop. They had to pay an extra 5.000,- DM for every seamstress. Today the following reckoning: Market value, turnover, profit, real estate etc. are added together, then 5.000,-€

are subtracted for each seamstress. There's not much left.

„Do it anyway, Paul. You have the comparison now, and know what is still worth doing in the German Federal Republic."

„I have to decide soon."

„All the better. Hello Paul, I have some more good news. Next week, although it's on Thursday, you will be visited by a Countess with her staff. The high nobility is taking notice of us. Get ready Paul."

„At your service your royal highness."

21

Major events cast a long shadow before them. Paul and his team, which was now augmented by Shark's sister, were waiting for a signal from the Countess. It was all to be kept a deep secret, including contractual penalties, if anything was leaked out to the public. But it also included a generous payment.

The contractual commitment also included no previous treatment for eight days prior to this, bathing three times a day two days before and washing with the supplied cosmetics etc. The day before, Paul, Rita and Sister Ingeborg had already arrived in the morning. The cleaning lady was booked. She had to use special cleaning products, Sister Ingeborg was responsible for the rooms. Was a special lounger needed for the countess? At least, there should be flowers in the waiting room.

Paul felt like the „Golden Calf."

The countess' secretary was expected that afternoon. She arrived punctually on the dot, in a severe navy blue tailored costume, with the family coat of arms on the lapelle. With her a typist, the countess deodorant and white towels with the family crest.

After three hours of intensive work, the secretary nodded condescendingly. She reminded everyone to be discrete and left with her entourage, leaving the deodorant and the white towels with the family crest behind.

Paul's little army was visibly impressed. Here, one thousand years of tradition looked down on them. They left, humbly saying goodbye.

The world, however, looked horizontal again the next day. They were ready for the entrance. As at court the parlour maid, about forty years old, entered first. She checked the practice once again thoroughly before reporting via cell phone to the noble camp.

Soon two stylish ladies in waiting arrived, somewhat grey but still in good shape. They checked Paul out intensely, again reporting back to headquarters.

The countess appeared soon after. Paul heard a lot of noise in the next room, including Ingeborgs deep voice, and then one octave deeper, was it the countess? Paul wanted to go out to greet her, but was stopped by the two ladies in waiting.

„Her ladyship wishes for no personal encounter.“

„Fine with me.“ Thought Paul.

More noise, then a group entered consisting, as of the introduction, of a doctor and two assisants into Paul's work area. Paul looked a little at a loss in his white bathrobe embroidered with the logo of the Hotel Krone. The doctor then got active, giving orders as if she were in her own practice. Pity Shark wasn't here. He would have told her off!

Still no sign of the countess, instead of which her animation team, the two ladies in waiting, began their business. They were pretty good. Could they have worked in a brothel earlier? Hardly! Had the old count been their teacher? More likely! Stupid stuff like this was going through Paul's mind. Meanwhile Elgar's Circumstances was playing. It wasn't easy to get a „hard-on" to that music. That was seen to by the two „ripe" girls. They were enjoying their work on Paul's Knight.

Alternating with hands and mouth, they woke the brave hero, driving him on, until the hero released a great stream of his juice. To be precise, the serum was collected in two venetian glass vases. Then, in no time, the two „girls" disappeared into the waiting room and all interest in Paul was gone. He now heard organ music. The countess absorbed his „heirs". Well, that was that. The countess and her entourage had disappeared. Fresh air!

What did she look like? She was veiled from head to foot, about sixty years old, with a deep voice, looking like clint eastwood's sister. What a to do. What for? For a lot of money.

22

„Here the secretary of Princess Fransiska von Luststone speaking.“

„Here the chancellor of the State Ministry for Unpublished Pornography.“

„Now, do you undertsand a subject's life?“

„At any rate, better than before.“

„Here the news bulletin from the Principality of Luststone: as we were satisfied with your services, we allow you to have your penis tattooed with a crown plus the word *Crown*, so that if you flag, it will read *Cow* instead, so you'll „cow down".“

„You envious ass. Normally it would read *Crown Jewel*.“

„And at full thrust of your Lafette: *Crown Jewel Guard*.“

„I'm sorry Shark, but nothing can cheer me up, I've sold my company and my concience is tormenting me.“

„Congratulations, the pain will fade. You'll soon be a wealthy man. Your chances of getting married are looking good!“

„Don't fool yourself. I didn't even get one tenth of the actual value. The number of workers cut the buying price down.“

„Just keep your penis up! The income has increased so much that I'm worried about the tax office. My accountant says that we should go for the whore's tax rate.“

„Isn't nursing service or medical assistance better?“

„That needs to be checked.“

„Can you imagine that the blow and handjobs really get me down sometimes? My hearts cries out for a simple, normal fuck! Do you understand?"

„You can do that in between."

„But, then I always think about the lost turnover."

„You inherited that from your mother. You had to pressure her to spend a deutsch mark or a euro."

Then, murmuring quietly. „She was a real cheapskate."

23

Tempora mutantur et nos in illis.
The times change, and we with them.

The good old company was gone. It wasn't his company anymore, just the skeleton of an image being scrapped bit by bit by the owners and the personell. He not only missed the work, but also the daily problems of his employees. He was headed into depression, in spite of his „Penis Success."

This had to be stopped. The two ladies of destiny, Marlisa and Rita joined forces to form a functoning union. As both were interested in Paul for different reasons, they soon found their areas of resposibilty, ideal for a coalition.

It was interesting to note that in all this time Rita had no idea of copulating with Paul. She had developed into a pilot fish for the Lamprade, luring new suckers. She gained tons of experience and had a highly interesting task at Paul's. She literally flourished in her profession.

Marlisa's interest was of a totally different nature. She was uncommitted and wealthy and had found her old love again. Now it was time to nurture and protect this happiness. Marlisa helped out more often in Paul's practice. For the future, should anything of Paul be left.

The slightest sign of weakness was immediately diagnosed and treated by two brains four hands and twenty fingures, and that mainly successfully.

The menue was given much more attention. Now, that they were able to afford more. Celery, caviar and oysters were now added to the diet.

Paul's „pipe" sparkled and bubbled away happily and steadily.

24

„Here Prince Brunzelfart's secretary."

„What's that supposed to mean Shark?"

„Something totally new. I got a phone call an hour ago. It was so rich in content, that I needed until now to digest and process it."

"Just admit it. Your brain isn't equipped for anything intricate."

„Whatever. Let me get right to the point. The firm Murkser-Chemicals called me! Professor Dr. Dr. Wormly, head of the developement department of pharmachology."

„And I hoped that my dick had developed brilliantly."

„And so it has. No one can get by your dick. They've heard about your monster. Apparently only good. Due to that Murkser did some research and the result was positive. So positive in fact, that they want to conduct a scientific examination in order to find and market a new compound against skin diseases."

„Am I also going to be asked about this?"

„I obviously negotiated in your favour. After all, we have a flourishing business here to be paused for this time frame."

„Can we afford this?"

„With the offer we got, certainly."

„We get 10.000,- Euros every week. This for approximately half a year. A positive result would lead to an increased figure that could reach hundreds of thousands. In case of an early termination on their part, and they will pay the following three months."

„Have you already agreed to it?"

„No way. All I said was. That is not enough! Yes, to the first three months."

„And their answer?"

„They're ready to negotiate."

„So, what do we do now?"

„They are coming to us for a detailed discussion."

„Thanks Shark, well done, I'm speechless."

„Me too."

25

They marched into town like aliens, right into Paul's and Shark's refugium. Up front, their leader Dr. Dr. Wormly, a bald headed, bloodless interlectual in his late 50's. He was accompanied by range of men and women, all of whom were obviously doctors, except for one more corpulent man. Mr Fettmann, the cook.

Prof. Dr. Wormly introduced them, and as it turned out: „Mr. Kolle Fettmann will take over your kitchen for the duration of our cooperation. He will be responsible for creating and cooking a dietry plan as consulted with us. It is up to you whether you want to keep your present kitchen help, or send her on vacation. We will obviously carry all costs. May I continue to introduce: This is Dr. Petkowitsch. She will be responsible for the hygiene in your home. Furthermore she will ensure that there is no sexual intercourse during this period, as previously discussed."

The Pharma company had thought of everything. Frau Dr. Petkowitsch was devoid of any feminine curves, she was pure spirit and as bodiless as a spray. Paul could rest easy.

„Have you put any other capacity onto me in my home?"

„Only if necessary! I do, however, recommend that our psychotherapist Dr. Aserbaidshan dip into the more intimate atmosphere of your home. Does that answer your question?"

Paul nodded, resigned to his fate.

The academians checked eveything for six hours. Then they got together for a compendium and Dr. Wormly ascertained: „The conditions that we have found here are certainly quite acceptable! The practice is clean and and accesable. The bathrooms are also in accordance with our hygienic regulations." Frau Dr. Tojibajew recommends new, better functioning fittings.We will fulfill her recomendations. Of course at our expense. Frau Dr. Spähling from the research department will be responsible for „Sperm-San", as this research test period has been named by us. She has the main key and will lock the door after a thorough cleaning is done and our labs are checked. She will also, obviously open the practice in the morning (Paul: at our expense). Further more, our internist, Dr. Tabachadse, will be available for your personal physical wellbeing. He will do a full check-up of the subjects an hour before and two hours after the seminal discharge. Herr Shark is allowed to examine our work once he has registered himself. Further questions of interest will be dealt with great care and discretion."

Finally, the expedition left the scene of „Sperm-San."

They left behind two stricken, exhausted men who asked themselves: „Did we do something wrong?"

26

„Hello Shark, are you still alive?"

„I think so. I just sold some aspirin in the shop. Selling aspirin means that I'm alive."

„Then give me a sanitorium-pack. Did we do the right thing? His horrible contract is seventeen pages long."

„True! But, who'll even look at it later? Things are never as bad as they seem. We can do this Paul!"

„I've heard that before."

„We have to go through with it. Let's get started!"

„You know what just came to mind?! Does the contract have an opting-out clause?"

„Good question! I don't remember any!"

„Then I can opt out at any time?"

„You don't really want to? I'm going to have a crisis! They didn't add any paprgraph because they're convinced that any reasonable man, which I'm convinced that you are, would forfit such a high salary. Paul we're talking hundreds of thousands! And now, of all times you have to develope dementia?"

„That's enough Shark. First I'll drown my problems in a female body. And, once he comes out, both he and the worries will be smaller."

27

Is was about dealing with the new cicumstances. To hand
over comand of the practice to the High Command was easier
than them taking over his private home. As it turned out, the
cook Kolle Fettmann, who in the presence of his superior Frau
Dr. Petkowitsch put on an arrogant attitude, afterwards turned
out to be quite relaxed and free of all pressure. He even had a
sense of humour and looked at his assignment as „time out" or
a short vacation.

To add to this, Paul's housekeeper Helga took a shine to
her new chef, and he to her. Cooking unites and is a turn on.
Where's the difference between preparing fresh chicken thighs,
veal filet or young venison, to be crumbed and larded, and the
foreplay of crispy young girls, hot women, mature ladies, all to
be tenderly washed, carefully creamed, to be devotely caressed?
Inevitably the teamwork got more intense and diverse. What
started out hesitantly on the kitchen hob and the kitchen table was later continued on the chaise longue and eventually
on all furniture providing the possibility of laying down. Cook
Fettmann had mutated into a ferret. Helga could handle it. Dr.
Petkowitsch the guardian of hygiene, caused no problem. Fun-
nily enough she turned out to be tolerant of the budding sex
games of her colleagues. Paul was proved right in the assump-
tion: This was the entree to a Menáge-a-trois.

Nevertheless, they got on his nreves. Wherever he was in the house, he was followed by Dr. Petkowitsch's shadow, meticulously observing his every movement. Paul suspected her of even checking on him in the toilet, after all it could be that he was selling the sperm, bought by her firm, on the free market through the toilet seat.

Stressed to such an extent, he went off to visit Rita's apartment. Through her new earnings, she had really done up her home.

Put together in Rita's style, it lacked the modern touch, but instead it was very cosy and comfortable and clean. They met there one midday. Marlisa joined them. They were celebrating „time off".

„Let's do something sensible with our free time."

Paul was somewhat surprised.

„Yes, something senselessly sensible!"

„We, that is to say, Rita and I think that you have no clue about women, let alone their sexual practices, for example: Foreplay! We, that's Rita and I, want to familiarise you with the art of how to treat women."

„Hush now, be quiet Paul, despite all your tenderness and size, we can make you better, isn't that what you also want?"

Paul wanted and was excited about what to expect. Rita excused herself for a minute, which she used to undress in her bedroom, but not completely, a silk sarong covered the nude lounging in a relaxed position, sensually on her wide bed. A soft smoochy music floated through the room. Marlisa attended to Paul. She undressed the surprised man and herself till there was little left and they entered the bedroom.

„Paul we're on a ship, Rita's ship and she's the captain.

What she orders, you must do! I am the „coxwoman", her deputy and know where we are headed to. You're the boatsman, you must obey. Clear?"

„Aye, aye coxwoman", shouted boatsman Paul.

„We are sailing on the endless Sea of Love!"

„Marlisa, I want to see more sea!"

„Shut up, you little sea-fetishist. Hello Boatsman, off to the captain's cabin!"

The ropes on the mainsail are overstrung! Loosen them. A tender kiss on the neck, then run your tongue slowly and very gently towards the ear. Now delicately use the fingers of your left hand, as it is more sensitive, then some gentle stroking with the fourth fingertip, even more gentle, almost imperceptable, but the captain will feel it! You can tell by her breathing! Now once more with the tip of your tongue, stay gentle please."

„And now the other side."

Paul changed position from Rita's buckboard to her starboard.

Thereby the ship started tilting.

„Careful, we're on a streamlined yacht. And now, the same procedure on the starboard side! We have plenty of time!"

„Let's move up to the prow, we're travelling on a catamaran, we have two breats that need careful maintanance if we're not to lose too much speed. Ahoi!"

28

„That's not possible", mumbled the elderly Herr Gimpel. „Something's not right."

Standing behind the window, covered by a curtain, he took his newly aquired binoculars for the umteenth time to observe the neighbourhood from left to right. To be more precise, he was watching the first floor of the four storied house number 27 opposite.

Gimpel could get himself so wonderfully agitated. Marga his wife, who was sitting in a downtrodden armchair behind the voyeur, groaned shortly and mumbled without interrupting her knitting for her grandson:

„Erich, are you serious? You get bent out of shape about everything, and are wasting our pension! Erich, were the binoculars really necessary?"

„Yes, a special offer at ALDI."

After a short break, hissing between his teeth:

„I'm going to find out!"

„What do you want to find out? There's nothing there."

Now, it's been over two years since he noticed something odd. He had noticed that the old tenants had moved out. Out of utter boredom he watched the new tenants move in. Very little was moved. But, then it got very lively over there. Obviously craftsmen. But why so many? They were changing everything. If I could only see better. Binoculars?

Gimpel was interested in everything, The great amount of time spent on moving in. In the mean time Gimpel had started a sort of diary and noted: Three men for six hours. Carpenters? Two men, electricians, three days for eight and one day for five hours.

Gimpel began calculating the labour costs. They must be loaded or at least earn a lot. Then the furniture arrived, armchairs, two loungers, wardrobes, so many modern lamps, oh God, think of the electricity bills. And, craziest of all, some sort of body, carried in by four men. It must have been really heavy. And the form, so curved? Could it be the statue of a dolfin? But then the movers took in rectangular fans. There were paintings, that was art!

Then two men showed up more and more frequently. The new tenants? Gay? No, there were two women, probably belonging to them and another one! Pretty glamorous ladies, my wrinkly Marga couldn't hold a candle to them.

Gimpel was now in a state of permanent excitement. He can't sleep anymore, in spite of downing more and more beers. Then, he sneaks into the neighbours house during working hours when he is less likely to be noticed. On the front door he discovers a newly attached sign „Dermatological Institute". Gimpel is a bit disappointed. After thinking about it, he asks himself, why not? Plucking up his courage, Gimpel climbs the stairs to the first floor. Everything is much finer than in our house. He doesn't use the elevator. Another little sign „Dermatological Institute". Very posh, or are they hiding something? While he is standing indecisively on the landing, the door opens, a man, one of the two, rushing past him to the stairs, stops shortly to ask Gimpel.

„Can I help you?"

Gimpel answers, „No thank you."

That had been his oportunity. He missed it! Gimpel reproached himself bitterly. But, what if the man had questioned him? Why? And then? Gimpel called the police. After listening to Gimpel's stuttering for a while, an inspector said:

„This is not enough to place a charge."

Gimpel, now left to his own devices, continued watching dilligently, and bought himself the binoculars from ALDI, on the „*Special*".

It wasn't easy, he discovered that there were very few visitors who each stayed for more or less an hour. What did they do? Nothing, the said room was facing the courtyard. A brothel? Should he stand watch at night?

„Erich, Erich, you're going too far, you're falling more and more into disrepair and turning into an alcoholic."

Yes, now it as getting more interesting. Minivans were arriving from Switzerland. Or were they from Heidelberg? What could it be? One object was different from the others. Everything looked so clean and technical. Were they building bombs here? Not simple carbombs, but rather, bombs that can blow up an entire government complex

Gimpels imagination was quite out of control. Gimpel marched off to the local „*Ordnungsamt*" (*regulatory office*), where a former aquaintance was working.

„No it's quite in order, everthing there is fine."

Gimpel is desperate. There are bombs being built and nobody seems to care. Should he break in, or blow the place up at night? Too late for that now, the alcohol has defeated him. Marga continues knitting busily away, the second grandchild has arrived.

She doesn't dive a damn about what happens to Erich or the neighbourhood.

29

There it was again, that restricting feeling, I have nothing more to say. A condition that he didn't like at all. That's why he hadn't liked going to school. You have to be punctual. You have to learn this and that, all the controlling. In principle the same condtions applied in this work-camp as in school or in the firm.

Being the boss! He could do what he wanted, when he wanted and how he wanted. That meant freedom to him.

Dear Paul that applied only to you, not to your employees.

He suddenly remembered: Paul, you don't have a company anymore, you took the feeling of being boss away from yourself. During these weeks, you have become one of those who follow orders.

An immense number of instruments were delivered two weeks prior to the start. One monstrosity in particular caught Paul's attention.

„This is our little refrigeration system. It's here to keep your sperm alive, it has to be deep frozen immediately."

Everything was pefectly organised, just like for a rocket launching. Paul's workdays were Monday, Wednesday and Friday. Work started punctually at 8am, as that is when men are most horny.

„The golden dawn, cums in the morn"

That was Dr. Spähling's sarcastic remark. Paul had another half an hour until his „*gold*" was all pumped out of him.

On the first day of production, both Dr. Dr. Wormly and Dr. Spähling approached Paul.

„How are we feeling today?"

Paul hated this patronizing, condescending doctor's greeting.

„I'm not well, how you are, you'll just have to find out for yourselves."

This was followed by a disapproving look, then a forced smile on both doctors lips.

„Now we have to lay hands on you. Frau Dr. Spähling will do this according to all mandatory hygienic precautions. Let's go!"

Paul lay on a super comfortable couch; his bathrobe slightly open, otherwise naked, awaiting Dr. Tojibajew's hands. They reached for Paul's still soft penis, when he heftily reacted.

„Not like that! You're wearing rubber gloves. It'll never work like this! Look what you've done to my dick! Look how it's shrunk."

„But, what about the hygiene, how can we gaurantee that?"

Dr. Dr. Wormly came and made a face. He was busy thinking.

„We can't lose the day. Let's try it without the gloves." said Paul, without looking at the doctors.

„What do we do now?" said Prof. Dr. Dr. Wormly.

And Paul went: „Rita has to come!"

Rita, a little later: „I knew it."

Everyone watching looked a little clueless and silly. Rita worked skillfuly, using her naked hand. Paul's fountain started splashing.

Everyone shouted „Thank God."

That was Monday. On Wednesday the regular players arrived again. Dr. Swellhand, a colleague of Dr. Tabachadse's, who was ill, came in beaming with joy. For many weeks at night he had been converting a milking-machine for cows into one for men. With the help of two men he pushed it into the room.

„I'm not doing that."

„Won't you at least give it a try?"

„Why don't you try it on yourself?"

Frau Dr. Spähling and her team looked at Dr. Swellhand.

„That's not a bad idea."

Dr. Swellhand had no choice. He and his helpers dragged the machine into the next room. The doors closed and soon a rattle was heard, which turned into a roar. This didn't last long. Were those screams of passion? Wow, heavy, and they didn't want to stop.

A quick thinking Paul rushed into the adjacent room. One look, a shock and Paul pulled the plug out of the wall.

And there was good old Swellhand lying on top of the machine. The team tried to free a terribly screaming Dr. Swellhand fom the grips of the machine. It was a hard job. Paul and Rita started to feel sick, they had to get out. They didn't see the rest of the mess. Dr. Swellhand's penis was torn behind the head, the foreskin was shredded and blood was flowing.

They passed up on Paul's daily production.

Dr. Swellhand didn't show himself. The healing took ages. When Dr. Swellhand finally returned to the masturbating copulating gang he was awarded the title of „*The One with the shredded Milkdick*".

30

„Did you?“

„I did!“

„I didn‘t see the end of it. I got sick. I stood in front of the toilet bowl, bent down and threw up.“

„That‘s teamwork, everyone giving his best.“

„All you contribute are stupid remarks and a stupid grin.“

„Accepted. But I haven‘t heard anything and I haven‘t read anything. Unbelievable, no article in the newspaper. Normally this would be a field day for the press. The Murksers are perfect. No blue light. „Pecunia non olet“ fits the toilet bowl and heals wounds.“

„They gave brave Swellhand one injecton after the other and even homeostasis to stop the bleeding. That calmed him down. Then off to the hospital.“

„Shark, that could have been me!“

„I already checked, according to the contract, the compensation would have lasted you to the end of your days.“

„Here we see your inhuman insensitivity! You‘re an emotionless dog!“

„Who love‘s reckoning.“

31

The next working day, Friday was slow and stagnant. Everyone was thinking about the previously so optimistic Dr. Swellhand, who was able to laugh so heartily. Now he was flat on his back. He had to undergo several operations before his penis could be brought back to it's natural shape. The problem was still the shredded foreskin. An experienced Jewish intern advised him to get the foreskin removed. But, the patient, a pious christian, was against this idea.

Everyone was wondering: would Dr. Swellhand ever be able to copulate again?

With these thoughts running through his mind, Paul lay on his large lounger while Rita fiddled with his penis. Frau Dr. Spähling suggested a hardcore porno film. Apparently she was quite experienced. A TV was fed with a DVD and the crew started avidly watching two wild threesomes; the way it should be, one with two men and one woman and the next with two women and one man.

Paul was pleased to see that his penis could compete in size and girth with the screen-fucker's. He also saw that Dr. Spähling's hand movements were rubbing wildly around and later in her pussy. All of that and Rita's increasingly stronger grip on his dick brought about the desired sperm release, comme il faut. During the team exclamation one could hear Dr. Spähling's coming through. She had managed an underhanded orgasm. Bravo!

The intermezzo with Rita went well for three weeks, was then exhausted and the coalition collapsed. Dr. Dr. Wormly was sympathetic

„I'll bring in a hostess."

Paul could not get rid of the feeling that he already had someone in mind.

„Now, get some rest until Monday. I have to go back to headquarters for a report, so I'll be back a day later."

Later Paul fell into a sort of agony: Just relax. To be alone! So, in the evening he wandered through the lonely streets. He was overcome by a strange shyness. Arriving at home he would listen to clasical music. Johann Sebastian Bach and especially the Goldberg Variations, alternating the interretations of Gould and Stadtfeld, which were the favourite CDs.

The following Monday passed in standby positon and nothing special happened. On wednesday, however, everyone felt that this was going to be a special week.

32

Dr. Dr. Wormly brought along not only a good mood, but an even better woman. What a hot number!

„Wow!"

„She's for Paul!"

„Oh!"

Now, the Professor wanted to inform the team and announce the first results.

„To start with, Herr Wieland's „*ejas*" (*ejaculations*) are all of the same quality. Furthermore: they contain the same amount of sperm, the same amount and consistancy of fluid, and most important, the same moveability. The lifespan is sufficient for the following experiments. It is approximately three hours and thirty seven seconds. We can work with that. Our delivery took one hour and forty minutes at minus thirty four degrees to reach the main lab at headquaters. 98% of the delivery is usable, which is an extremely high percentage. The main lab is in a good mood and they hope to soon be able to show accountable results. They want me to give you their heartiest regards. Keep it up!"

Clap, clap, clap, a lasting round of applause.

Paul felt like Uncle Johann's cow Lotte during this speech. As a boy he used to spend his school holidays in the country with Uncle Johann and Aunty Lisbeth.

„Good girl Lotte, just milked another bucket of milk. Good

girl, pat, pat, pat, stroke, stroke, stroke! Good boy Paul, the glass is fully milked, pat, pat."

At this moment Paul sat staring like Lotte the cow. How the images resemble one another. (Opera Tosca by uncle Johann, rubbish, Giacomo Puccini, keep it up!)

33

Lascivious thoughts were reflected in Paul's head. He thought of the „Crazy Horse" looking at the beauty before him. The positive mood of success was transfered onto Paul and the team, who were now like a conspirator's circle. Then Paul awoke from his old Sex-dreams. It was time to get to work.

The „O" lady called herself Plis. Having grown up in the Czech Republic, she finished her „fine tuning" in Paris. At first she looked bored and disinterested. After all she was one of those „private girls" meant for doctors, directors, board members and chairmen.

Her attitude switched instantly the moment she saw Paul's dick. Her body tightening up, just like Paul's „little one". The panther in her awakened. Prof. Dr. Dr. relaxed the tension.

„Just be nice and gentle with one another and start; it's going to be fine."

Further utensils were no longer necessary. The new and „new" were quite sufficient. The „suction pump" was turned on and her expert fingers brought Paul to a prompt ejaculation.

„Very convincing", as Dr. Dr. put himself in Paul's position.

Paul murmered „too bad" and was ready to leave.

They were done for the day. Great! It worked well for eight days, then both Paul and Plis began to show signs of wear and tear. It took longer and longer. Then both, as from the same lips.

„We can't go on like this!"

Prof. Dr. Dr. Had no option but to allow a breathing space. This lasted another eight days. Then she called the professor.

„Hermann, can't I bring Okumi with me?"

„I'll have to think about it", and to his colleagues at headquarters:

„Can we „up" our expense account?"

After work began again the following week, Prof. Dr. Dr. Wormly announced proudly:

Hear, hear, we've achieved an amazing success: The ground substances have been found. We can build the serum from the chain of elements.

Plis appeared accompanied by her friend Okumi. Quietly smiling to herself.

„Very sexy" remarked Paul. She was coffee brown and equipped with that special Booty (backside) that he had always wanted. Her in the coffe brown leather chair in his office would look great. Then he remembered: the company and the chair no longer existed for him.

At first everything went just fine. There was a lot of laughter. Paul, like a never ending fountain, splashed sweet poerty into the two bewitched sex-fairies ears and sperm into the little glasses, without   lack of attention to the two beauties.

But then, what had to happen happened. Habit is the killer of love, sensuality and effusion. They were faced with the decision: after the hand and oral jobs, whether to introduce the final step. Or? And so, Prof. Dr. Dr. finally agreed. How could Plis and Okumi ruin Paul anyway? It fits: a good sable in a beautiful vagina! Final success was just around the corner.

Once again things were really good and diversified for Paul, even though his good stuff ended up in a container instead of inside a trembling woman's body. The two animating ladies had great fun with Paul's toy, surprising him by changing positions and getting themselves involved in the game, turning it into a hot threesome. Prof Dr. Dr. Wormly was thoughtful about whether they would notice it at Headquarters, which they did and wrote. The intensity of the ejaculation had been strengthened. How did you manage this?

Paul thought that the women's hormones had sprung onto his penis connecting with his sperm, acting as a catalyst.

Great! It would be best if Marlisa knew nothing of this. As he was now miming the exhausted man, sick of being constantly milked.

34

„Hi there, Paul."

„Hi there, Shark. What's up, anything special?"

„What makes you think that?"

„The unusual form of greeting."

„Paul, the bloodhound in you! Still functioning! Guess what happened? First, I heard some mumbling over the phone. It turned out that the Gibberish was English. The next surprise: it turns out that I had the private office of Abu ibn Karim, an Emirate on the Persian Gulf, on the line. The conversation to be kept absolutely secret, obviously under the threat of the death penalty....."

„Shark? Under what? What are we supposed to keep secret? Will heads roll? Yours, mine, possibly both of ours?"

„For a few weeks now, the Sheikh's young Harem-wife has been suffering from a bad skin condition in her private area. The spots appear to have seriously lowered the Sheikh's desire. Every medical capacity has been trying to help her pussy. No healing. Now it's your turn. Your reputation blows from oasis to oasis and right to the Emirate of Abu ibn Karim."

„Do I play the role of the camel here?"

„That has yet to be determined."

Shark, you camel driver, we have responsibilities. We're under contract to the concern."

„Exactly! I've already mentioned this problem."

„And, the reaction?"

The Arab isn't interested. „We're all easily shaken by a Sheikh".

All those notes turn us into billigoats. They pay well, so Basta!"

„This could get hot. Also, end up a fiasco. Do you have the concerns answer yet?"

„Not yet. Things take forever in that place. And the Sheikh is in a hurry. He wants to be fucking again and is only in Germany for a few days."

„I sense something bad. This could get stormy!"

„I sense something worse. This could be a sandstorm!"

„Should we inform the police for our protection? Or the Arabian embassy?"

„Or the Minister of the Exterior."

„Or, put our heads in the sand."

„There's a sandbox outside in the courtyard, but only kids are allowed to put their heads in the sand."

„God be with us. But, with whom?"

„Paul don't be scared. I'm with you!"

35

The „developement" department was intensely doing it's job. Everything was working smoothly, like a charm, fully concentrated. Suddenly, strange noises that definitely didn't fit into the rythm of science, were heard at the door to the apartment. Crashing noises and a full BANG. The door to the practice-room was thrown open and in the door-frame stood two gigantic men, unnecessarily emphasizing their superiority with the pistols in their hands. Why? Just for a little sperm? Yes, but Paul Wieland's! Apparently he was worth it!

Paul and his hostesses noticed the rest of the team laying flat out on the floor, all knocked out! A third guy, the leader and spokesman of the Abu ibn Karim riot squad stood there ordering:

„Paul and the fuck-girls, continue, we need Paul's sperm for Fatima(Emirate, Abu ibn Karim), suddenly and warm!"

It was almost a miracle of Fatima (of Lourdes) that Paul with the help of his women was able to serve the desired „warm" as required. One of the guards, Omar Caijam, looking into the glass, measured the sperm and to Paul's horror shouted:"That's all? Once again!" Pistols were waved. Paul was in trouble. He had his reasons, the huge man wanted to grab Paul's, or rather the donors dick, but was immediately stopped by his companions. Having laid down his gun, he was now jacking off at the sink, without taking his eyes off Paul. Obviously, Paul was bothered by his staring. He was less bothered by the other man whose trousers were down while he was fucking Plis from Paris from behind. Even later after Paul had delivered his dues. But, everything comes to an end. Lady „O" was paid double for working double.

Even as the last throws of work were in progress, the sound of police sirens, ambulance and even the fire brigade could be heard. Right after, the local police stormed into the practice:

„Hands up!"

There were screams, shouting and helpless gesticulations until Paul shouted:

„Stop. Stop!"

It took some time for the gun flapping hands to calm down and it took even longer for all involved: the developement-director, the police inspector with his masked entourage, the reporters and the rest, to realise how comforting and convincing two or three little cases can be. Money is a well proven medium that calms, convinces, against and with reason and against and with unreason.

With oaths and affirmation they came to a cinematic ending. All that was missing was the clap-board: *The End.*

36

„Paul. Have you not been fucked to death?"

„No, Shark, just missed death. This cannot happen again."

„I know it was awful. I was there, I was one of the KO's in the waiting room laying on the floor."

„Shark, that's only fair. After all you're part of the business."

„I know. Paul? They didn't give us a chance. Did you see our establishment after the sandstorm? An indescribable chaos , but after a quick investigation, I found out that most of the apparati are fine. The damage is minimal."

„Then we can continue, once the shock therapy on our doctors is over. That could take some time."

„What amazes me: nothing in the press, inspite of all the police and cars blocking the street."

„Shark, it was all hushed up with cash."

„To get back to the danger. They won't come back, will they? You're living dangerously. Now that you're known to the police, I suggest you get a new passport under another name."

„That would be the best, and soon. Thank God the skin tests have been successful so far."

„Paul, they still need you. Keep the fountain flowing."

„But not just the concern, Marlisa is waiting. Shark, I've been thinking. My last Will! As a friend, I want to do something for you. While I was having fun with the prettiest chicks, you were left alone with your fantasies staring into space. I'll speak to the two sweet girls. Maybe they'll make an exception for your dick. It'll have to happen here in the lab with no supervision. I'll come up with something!"

„Thanks Paul."

37

Our scientists met up at Paul's place two months later to end the experimental series.

The concern had filtered out the serum and were now able to reproduce it chemically.

„They're in the process of producing drops and ointments in different concentrations. They had done repeated tests on individuals with skin conditions from the beginning, comparing the results with the previous patients. The developement department was very satisfied with their progress. They didn't even hesitate for long after the attack, the project still seemed to be extremely profitable. They are expecting the final result to be released in a couple of months. It was now time to match the previous method with the up and coming one."

There was no avoiding it, the end was near. They all seemed a little sad. Paul was in a daydream. It had been just like a holiday, everything so harmonious; for example the slapping of moist thighs, the giggling of the avid girls and their screams of pleasure, the blissful moaning of the more mature women, the rattling of the instruments, half whispered words and ending up with a glass of prosecco or champagne. All of this should come to an end.

With a provisional clause, attached to a due compensation, Paul the Healer should no longer exist. Why not? Paul had seen to it that he, Marlisa, Shark and Rita were financially secure for the rest of their lives.

One could calmly await the up and coming negotiations.

„Of course it all turns out differently than one would expect.“

Professor Dr. Dr. Wormly head of the devlopement department of Murkser Chemicals, thus opened his discourse. What did it mean? It was like a funeral.

„Surprisingly and unexpectedly our child Dermosan passed away at birth. It was not able to partake of the events of this world and the joy of living.“

The drug „money“ prevented it's transition into into commercial life. In other words, the large concern Murkser Chemicals received an offer from an association consisting of almost all pharmacutical and cosmetic companies worldwide, that stilled the newly born's first breath. It concerned an offer that would also mean a huge amount for Paul and Shark. It took them quite a while to stop gaping and finally whisper their „yes“.

Answering Shark's question as to whether the „association“ would maybe participate in the production.

„Where from? The patent will be locked in a safe with all it's documents. Everything stays the way it was. The compensation is so much higher than we could ever have earned with the new product. Our work has really paid off.“

39

„Hello Paul?“

„Hello Rita!“

„Thank you so much! That was some supplement. You‘re the best boss I ever had.“

„Rita you only had one boss.“

„Only one.“

„Thank you. What are your future plans?“

I‘m a Lamorade, remember? I have sucked onto a strong man-fish. We want to get married.“

„Congratulations! Think about your children. What‘ll you do if they get acne?“

„I‘ve already thought about that. Prof. Dr. Dr. Wormly was so kind as to send me a little bottle of healing serum from the lab.“

A little later.

„Hello Shark.“

„Hello pensioner.“

„What have you got planned? Are you remaining a pharmacist?“

„I‘m not sure. The next question is, what do we do with the money?“

„Invest in property. That seems to be fairly safe for the future. And you?“

„I‘m still torn between a few ideas. I may stay in touch with the Murksers, open a „Murkser Branch", or keep the institute going, for example „Fuck for Health". Or maybe sex-consulting for misunderstood women. „Misunderstood? We Stabilise". Maybe even write a book, a porno; „Sucked in by Passion".

„That should suit you you old pig. Yes that'll suit you. By the way Marlisa and I are getting married next month. You'l be getting an invitation."

„By the way, I'm getting married as well."

„Were you born in March?"

„Yes, why do you ask?"